Sadie's Trade

LATTER-DAY DAUGHTERS

BOOKS IN THE LATTER-DAY DAUGHTERS SERIES

Sadie's
Trade

LATTER-DAY DAUGHTERS

Launi K. Anderson

Published by
Deseret Book Company
Salt Lake City, Utah

To John H. and Agnes P. Kirby

whose lives taught us to

walk uprightly

Library of Congress Cataloging-in-Publication Data

Anderson, Launi K., 1958–
   Sadie's trade / by Launi K. Anderson.
     p.   cm. — (The Latter-day daughters series)
   "Cinnamon Tree."
   Summary: While her parents attend a meeting aimed at reforming their lives as Mormons in Utah in 1856, twelve-year-old Sadie takes charge of her brothers and sisters on the family farm.
   ISBN 1-57345-415-X
   [1. Mormons—Fiction. 2. Brothers and sisters—Fiction.
3. Frontier and pioneer life—Utah—Fiction. 4. Utah—Fiction.]
I. Title. II. Series.
PZ7.A54375Sad   1998
[Fic]—dc21
                                        98-33733
                                            CIP
                                            AC

Printed in the United States of America   21239-6415

10   9   8   7   6   5   4   3   2   1

"Saints, live your religion."

BRIGHAM YOUNG

CONTENTS

CHAPTER ONE

Having a Spell

"First word," Ginny said, "*Orchard.*"

The blossoms in Carters' apple orchard came on so thick last spring that when I squinted my eyes and stared out at them, I  could believe they were really pink and white divinity trees—easy. It was all I could do not to pick the flowers and taste them, just to be sure. But the bees worked over those buds so heavy we were obliged to go *around* the orchard altogether, instead of through, to keep from getting stung.

See the glossary at the end of this book for an explanation of unusual words and expressions marked with an asterisk (*).

Writing the letters in the air with my spoon, I said, "O-R-C-H-A-R-D."

"Anella and Willard had better thin out those apples," Pa said. "They won't be worth a mule's hindquarters if they don't."

"Watch your language around the children," Ma said as she plopped a mound of cereal in each bowl. "And just how would that poor old couple ever thin out those trees? They'd be sick for a month if they tried."

I smiled to myself. It's always this way: Pa fretting over the neighbors' crops and Ma fretting over the neighbors.

"Give me the next word, Ginny."

She looked at Ma, then Pa. She worries too much.

I tapped the book to remind her that we were studying.

At last she said, "*Garret.**"

"J-E-R-A-A-U-N-T-V-M-X-Y-Z," Preston teased.

It was Friday again, and Miss Stevens was expecting me to do well in the spelling bee. After all, I'm one of her best spellers.

"What would you like me to do?" Pa asked, eating a spoonful of mush. "I can't tend to our farm and theirs too. You know that."

I crossed my eyes at Preston. "G-A-R-R-E-T," I spelled.

"Right," Ginny said. It's a good thing for me that my little sister takes nearly as much pride in seeing me win as I do.

Preston—now, that's another story.

We get along well enough as brothers and sisters go, but he doesn't care much for schooling. The spelling bee is the furthest thing from his mind. It's the *only* thing in mine. I aim to win the "Big Match"* this year if I have to wear myself out trying.

"*Adobe.*"

Ma held the kettle out to one side and put her other hand on her hip, so it was certain she meant business. "If we were any kind of neighbors at all, we'd get over there and help the Carters."

"A-D-O-B-E."

"Edie, we got enough to do . . ." Pa never got further than a few words once Ma started one of her tirades,* unless she got mad enough to stomp right out of the house, which she didn't do very often.

"Solomon Russell, just look at these likely* children sitting here no better than a load of firewood.* Preston, Sadie, Ginny. I've never seen so many people afraid of hard work in all my life. Why, even baby Jake could help some. It makes me ashamed."

"I'm five," Jakey wailed. "I'm not no baby."

Ma ignored him, went back to the hearth, and set the kettle down hard.

Pa wobbled his head and raised a face at us kids. He always does that when Ma's going on. She'd probably never even notice he was doing it, except he makes us laugh every time. Well, all but Ginny. She frowns because she thinks we're being mean to Ma.

Of course, nobody's *that* brave.

Before I had three mouthfuls down, Ma turned and started waving her arms at us. "Get out of here, all of you. I don't need you making fun of me. There's chores to be done."

Keeping an eye on her and the pan of sugar biscuits in her hand, I gulped down a big swallow of milk and grabbed my grammar book. Tucking it under my arm, I squeezed past Preston, who was already moving for the door.

"Go on now, get!" Ma said, pointing toward the porch and stomping her foot.

Ginny and Jakey just sat still, 'cause Ma never meant *them*.

Pa grabbed up a piece of meat and stuffed it into his mouth, grinning and making like any minute Ma was going to whack him. He joined us outside just in time to hear something hit the door.

Preston, still chewing, said, "Pa, just once I wish you'd let us finish breakfast before you got Ma started."

"Sorry, son," Pa said, smiling. It was plain to see he wasn't a bit sorry. "Your Ma sure is a spitfire.* I'll say that. Anybody daring enough to see what that was hitting the wall? I didn't get one of her biscuits this morning."

Both Pa and Preston turned my direction.

I backed to the porch rail, shaking my head. "Don't neither of you go looking over here. Last

5

time I tried sneaking back in, I got the mush
stick* thrown at me."

Pa, looking all thoughtful, said, "I suppose we
better learn to eat faster."

CHAPTER TWO

Robber's Run

Once those blossoms had burst into fruit and started redding up,* Preston and I found no trouble thinning them. In fact, we helped a little every morning before school. It just wasn't the way Ma had intended.

Preston always sent Ginny on ahead, saying we wanted to wash up some at the spring and that we'd be along directly. We both knew she couldn't be trusted to keep quiet. No nine-year-old can. Ginny was at that age where, no matter how far away she went, she still had a hold of Ma's hand. Ginny couldn't be trusted, not yet.

"Reach your skirt out bigger," Preston said, tossing down two apples at a time, "and mind you, don't miss none."

I caught them both in my apron. "You just pay attention to how you drop them, 'cause if you hit me in the head again, I'll tell Ma."

"Oh yeah, Sadie? What'll you tell her?" He started talking in a high-pitched voice like Jakey does when he cries: "'Ma, we were swiping some of Sister Carter's apples this morning and that bad old Preston, he hit me in the head with one.' That'd be a fine way to get us both hit in the head. How will you win the spelling match then?"

I couldn't help laughing, even if he was making fun of me. "Just hurry. I'll do the catching all right, *and* the spelling."

"I'm going up higher," he said, swinging one arm around the branch just above him and hoisting himself onto it. "There are some real big ones towards the top."

The rustling and snapping of the tree limbs always made me nervous. I wasn't so scared that Press would get hurt bad. Not him. Inside and out, he's made of bear hide.

It's just that if we busted up the branches, it'd be plain that some rascal had been up there.

Ma never said anything if we took the cast-off* fruit from the ground, but she said it wasn't the same as picking the trees outright. So we figured it best to leave as little trail behind us as possible.

"Preston, we've got more than we can eat already. Come on, or we'll be late for school."

"Sadie, quit squawking. You're starting to sound like an old crow."

I let the five apples in my apron roll to the ground. Then, holding my arm up to block the morning sun, I tried to glare at him. Before I could say that I was gonna leave him here if he didn't hurry, the biggest, reddest, shiniest apple—a real beauty—came barreling out of the leaves heading straight for my face. I tried to duck, but it hit me like a brick right on the forehead, then bounced down to the ground.

"Ow! Darn you, Preston!" As bad as it hurt, I'd have to say I was more mad than wounded. I rubbed at the knot growing on my head while the

apple sat in the grass, looking all pretty and inno-
cent.

There he stood in the tree, grinning like a
circus monkey. "Why, Sadie, did I just hear you
curse? Wait till I tell Ma."

"You won't have a chance if I get my hands on
you," I hollered and started up after him. Just as
I got myself steady between the first two limbs, I
heard a woman's voice from far off. It was hard to
make out what she was yelling, but it didn't matter much, seeing as how she was headed this way.

"It's Sister Carter," Preston said. "We're gonna
catch it now. Move, so I can jump."

"You can't jump from there." I pulled at my
foot. It had wedged itself tight in the lowest
crook.* With one hard yank I jerked it free, but
tore the leather sole away from the toe clear to the
middle of my shoe.

"You there! Get out of those trees!" Sister
Carter called.

"Move, Sadie!" Preston shouted.

I snatched up my books, leaving the apples
behind, and took off at a run. I heard my brother
hit the orchard grass right where I'd been stand-

10

ing seconds before. I could tell he landed hard by the thud and the "dang!" he let out before he came running behind me.

Despite my struggle to keep from tripping on the flap hanging beneath my foot, I still beat Press to the clearing, which had never happened before that I could recall.

We stopped running near Dr. Dunyon's place to catch our breath, then walked the rest of the way to the schoolhouse. Inside, Pearly Fletcher was already reciting from her reader. Something about a girl putting her dolls into a paper boat and sending them down the river.

With one look at us, Miss Stevens let out a gasp like someone had slapped her dog, which made the whole classroom turn around. Other than the fact that we were late again, and that Pearly always gawked at Preston, I couldn't figure why everyone was staring so.

Ginny's eyes were as big as silver dollars.

With one glance at my brother, I realized how mauled* we had to look. Me, with the goose egg on my head and shoe sole dragging; and Press, with dirt rubbed across the front of his shirt and a long tear in one sleeve. Up until that moment, I hadn't noticed that he was limping too.

When Miss Stevens asked what on earth had happened to us, I sighed and slid into my regular seat, knowing Preston would make up some story—just like he always did.

He went on about how we had fallen down by the river, gotten all banged up, and ran all the way so's we wouldn't be late for school.

The teacher made a strange face at the both of us, probably because if we'd been by the river, by rights we should be a little wet. Of course, we weren't.

The funny thing was that Preston's "stories" are usually so much better than the one he told, I think even Miss Stevens was disappointed. I know *I* was.

CHAPTER THREE

Robber's Roost

Zeke and Hal Walker fashioned Press a crutch at lunchtime, but Ginny and I still had to help him home. He kept on acting like he twisted his ankle down by the river because of Ginny being there, but I knew it happened when he jumped from the tree.

Once we got him up the steps, he told us to back away so he could try to walk regular-footed into the house. Lucky for us, Ma was busy cutting Jakey's hair, 'cause on his first step Press winced so bad, I was sure he was gonna yell.

I made a move to steady him, but he shook his head enough to set me still. Just before Ma looked to the doorway at us, he took a deep breath, pretended to smile, and walked right in.

"Children," she said, snipping a stray lock and letting it fall to the floor, "you're home."

"Yes," I said, following Press to the stairs.

"So, how did the practice match go?"

The three of us looked up at the steep incline that led to our bedroom. Press shook his head, letting us know he couldn't make it up the steps.

"Fine, Ma," I called. Knowing what her next question would be, I gave her the answer before she asked. "Murial Jacobs came in first."

We decided the easiest place to rest him and his foot would be in Ma and Pa's room, on their husk mattress.* Once we got out of Ma's sight, he grabbed onto the door and held fast. He closed his eyes like he hoped to faint, but I knew he wouldn't.

"You all right, Press?" I whispered.

"I suppose so," he said, blowing out his breath as if it was the last he had. We helped him hobble over and sit back on the bed. Little drops of sweat were starting to shine on his forehead.

"I never seen anybody so brave as you, Press," Ginny said, acting like she was gonna cry.

Ginny cries over almost everything.

"And all so's you don't worry Ma."

"Or get a lickin', you mean," I said.

Press fired a look at me fast as a bullet, then softened up and said, "Ginny, she means 'cause I tore my shirt."

"What place did *you* get, Sadie?" Ma called.

For a second, I didn't know what she meant. Then I remembered: the spelling bee. I sighed. "Fourth, Ma."

"Ma can fix your shirt," Ginny whispered. "Besides, when she sees how hard you're trying not to worry her, she'll be proud of you, too."

Preston smiled at me. "Don't go getting too sappy on me now, Gin."

I rolled my eyes, grateful for once that this nine-year-old didn't think too hard.

We'd sooner catch a weasel asleep than fool Ma, though. I just got Press situated on the straw mattress when he looked past me and said, "Hello, Ma."

When I turned, there she stood in the doorway, with Jake hanging on her dress. He saw the bump on my head right off and pointed, saying, "Ooooooh, Sadie," over and over.

"Sadie," Ma said, "what are you children doing in here? Preston, are you feeling sick?"

She wasn't too pleased when she got a good look at my forehead.

Frowning, she said, "Have you children been fighting? Well? Who's gonna answer me?"

For once, Preston had nothing to say—and try as I might, I couldn't make any words come out, either. All I could do was stand there with my mouth gaping open like a fish.

Ginny, half-smiling as if she knew a great secret, said, "No, Ma, they weren't fighting. Press and Sadie were washing up at the spring this morning and had an accident."

I nodded for her to go on, relieved that she wanted to give the story. It's always easier for me to listen to a lie—no matter who it belongs to— than to be the one telling it.

"Sadie slipped and hit her head on a rock. Then Preston twisted his ankle trying to help her."

"Sadie fell down," Jakey chanted, "and broke her crown."

I cleared my throat and glared at him until he hid behind Ginny.

Ma came to the side of the bed, acting more irritated than worried. First she glanced down at Preston. Then she took a hold of my face at the cheekbones with one hand and tilted my head to better light. While checking the bump, she said, "I'd like to know what kind of rock did this, Sadie?"

It was hard to answer with my mouth pinched up in her hand, but I managed to mumble, "A great big one."

Pursing her lips, she said, "Uh huh." She didn't sound convinced.

At last, she turned me loose and took a hold of Preston's boot.

He braced himself like he was biting a strap as she tugged and pulled until it came off.

What a sight that foot was! It's a wonder we didn't have to cut his shoe off, for it was half again as big* as the other foot. Preston's ankle bone was nowhere to be seen under all the swelling. It was

17

purple and dark from the underside of his heel to his shin—worse than what I'd expected.

"Glory almighty, boy," Ma said.

I looked up into her face, thinking suddenly that her words sounded tired and old.

I wanted to say, "Preston will be fine, Ma," or touch her arm or something, but I didn't. I just stared at Preston's ankle, then back at Ma.

Straightening up, she said, "Ginny, run for Dr. Dunyon. Tell him to come ready to set this leg. I'd say it's broken. Jakey, you go play in the yard."

Ginny stood still for a second or two, then took Jake's hand and ran out the door.

Ma set to work making a poultice,* which stunk to high heaven. She packed it in a cloth strip around Preston's foot.

I just stayed out of the way while Ma moved around the room from the stove to the bed, almost like she was waltzing. Even with her hair falling from the coil at the back of her neck, and the terrible worry on her face, she looked pretty to me. I almost found myself envying Press for the attention he was getting.

By the time the doctor came through the door, my brother was nearly asleep—and the poultice was due for a change.

Dr. Dunyon was a kindly fellow with smiling crinkles around his eyes. He had more hair on his chin than his head. He hadn't been in Pleasant Grove a year, but already the townsfolk had taken to him.

Without saying a word, he set his black case down on the rocker in the corner of the room and carefully began examining Preston's ankle. The room was quiet but for Ginny's sniffing and Pa's old clock ticking on the bed table.

At last, turning to Ma, he said, "It's broken all right, Edith. How he ever got home on it, I'd like to know."

He's made of bear hide, that's how, I thought.

"I'll get it set and splinted," Doc said, "but he's gonna have to stay off of it for a month or so, or it won't heal properly." Looking down at his patient, he said, "You understand my meaning, young man?"

Preston nodded.

Giving me half a smile, the doctor said, "So, young lady. Just how high was this apple tree?"

Chapter Four

Last Straw

It seems that for all our running, Sister Carter had seen us plain as day and knew just who had been robbing her trees all this time. Seeing Dr. Dunyon for her rheumatism,* she'd told him all about it.

Now, Ma is mostly fair with misbehaving children, and usually what we get is what we have coming. But the very idea of her two oldest children leading everyone through a pack of fibs, especially Miss Stevens, had Ma fit to be tied.

Preston lay in bed, not having to take the full heat of Ma's anger because he was now an invalid. I guess everyone felt like his crime and his punishment were well matched. However, my head bruise didn't seem to be serious enough to keep me from getting my share of the wrath—and Preston's share, too.

Ma went through little patterns of mad to where she'd holler things like, "What were you two thinking?" or "Your Pa will sure hear about this," and then she wouldn't speak to me at all. I wasn't sure which I liked better. The yelling was hard, but the quiet was almost worse. It was certainly noisier, because Ma would walk around in a huff, stomping and banging dishes till I was sure she was gonna break something.

In the middle of one of the yelling times, I looked over to Preston to see if he might be feeling bad for me at all. Not only was he not worried, he had somehow fallen asleep. It was all I could do not to jiggle the bed hard.

Finally, when Pa did come from the field, I was so fretful waiting and worrying about what he'd do, I just hoped he'd get the scolding over with fast. I had hoped that Ma would give me time to tell him about the spelling bee so he could be proud a few seconds before being ashamed. But she heard his footsteps on the porch and went outside, determined to tell him the whole sad story before he got one foot in the door.

To my relief, after hearing the tale, he just chinked his mouth to one side and shook his head at me and Press. I expected a lecture, but it didn't come. Instead, Pa caught his heel on the bootjack* and let his boots fall to the floor. Without even putting them in the corner, he came over to the bedside and stared down at Preston laying there all dead-like.

"Something's got to change," he said. "This ain't right."

"What are you talking about, Sol?" Ma said.

Pa rested his hand on Preston's forehead, making him stir a bit, then moved back and sat in the rocker. It took a minute, but finally he looked up at Ma and said, "Do we believe, Edie? I mean, do we truly still believe?"

Ma and I exchanged confused looks, but neither of us spoke.

"Listen," Pa said. "Today I rode out to check the stock and found that six of our cattle and two mares crossed through a bad gap in the fence. They have been grazing in Brother Richardson's pasture for some time now. He feels that since the animals have been feeding off his land, they now belong to him. He has even branded them."

"What can we do?" Ma asked.

"I suppose I could talk to the bishop. But Edie, don't you see? That's not the point. No one seems to know what's right and wrong anymore. People—Latter-day Saints—take what doesn't belong to them. They're lying and cheating each other. We're members of the Church and ought to know better. How long's it been since we've had regular meetings on Sunday? Why, even our own children . . ."

He stopped and sunk his head into his hands.

Though I felt small enough to fit into a mouse hole, I couldn't take my eyes off Pa. I'd never seen him act this way. In fact, I couldn't remember Pa ever getting ruffled over much of anything.

Ma didn't seem to know how to take Pa's behavior either, so she just stood by him with her hand on his shoulder.

At last, he said, "Something needs to be done. We're gonna start making some changes. I heard

Brother Jacobs say that there is a conference in Salt Lake City next week. We should go listen to the prophet speak. It might be just the kick in the pants this family needs."

Ma squinted her eyes a bit. "We can't leave now. There are potatoes to dig, corn to shell,* and Sadie and I are making soap next week. With Preston down, we'll already be short on help."

"Let it go, Edie," Pa said. "Come with me. Either we intend to live the gospel or we don't."

Ma stared at him slow and steady. "Someone's got to have sense about running this place. Besides, I couldn't leave the children when Preston needs taking care of."

I was glad she didn't want to go. How would we manage without her here? If Preston was well, then maybe. But with him down, all the work would fall to me. I didn't like the sound of that much.

"We'd look after him, Ma," Ginny said. "You should go with Pa. We'll be all right, won't we, Sadie?"

That girl. "Hush, Ginny," I said. "Ma can make up her own mind."

25

"Edith, it's only two days," Pa said. "I'm asking you to come with me."

Jake came down the stairs heading straight for Ma. He grabbed onto her skirt and cried, "Don't go, Ma. Don't."

Ma looked like she was being pulled to pieces. "Solomon, why do you do this to me?"

"It's for our family," he said. Then, looking straight at me, he said, "We'll get this train back on track yet."

CHAPTER FIVE

The Trip

The week before they left for Salt Lake City, Ma and Pa kept us busy. Pa said that since the corn shelling and soap making would have to wait until he got back, the best we could do would be to bring in as many of the potatoes as we could. They'd take the extra into town on this trip.

Potato digging is hard work all by itself, never mind trying to do it in a hurry. We hoed until my back ached and the skin of my right hand was sore and raw—and still, we kept on.

I sure missed working alongside Preston. At least he could keep us laughing. Ginny was a slow digger, and all Jakey did was whine and toss more dirt into the wagon than potatoes.

It really bothered me that Ma and Pa were leaving. I mean, what was I going to do with all these children to tend?

I talked for two days and nearly had Ma convinced to take Jakey with them—so I could study my words, I said. After all, the Big Match was coming up in one month.

Then Ginny spoke up again about how she'd just love to tend him.

When I got her alone I told her, "It won't be you that does the tending. It'll be me. So keep quiet."

It was too late. Ma had decided that she'd never hear any of conference at all if she brought him along.

"Sadie," she said, "if you're worried about being here alone, I can always ask Sister Carter to check up on you. I'm sure she wouldn't mind."

And have her mingling with the very apple thieves that had robbed her only one week ago? Oh, no, I thought. Under the circumstances, I was forced to say, "We'll be fine, Ma," though I doubted if that was true.

It was also an irritation that Preston was inside

the house whittling away his time while we were all out here working.

The more I thought about it, the madder I got. Until it seemed the potatoes were coming up much easier and I was tossing them behind me with great force. At least anger can make a person work fast.

Then I saw Pa coming around the back of the wagon. He was wiping his face with his kerchief and brushing dirt from his shoulders.

"Sadie," he said, sounding like he was mad himself.

"Let's just have you go inside for a while, shall we?"

"But Pa, I just started getting good," I said.

"The last two potatoes you threw hit me in the back. The ones before that came so fast that I had to duck to keep from getting killed. Now, go into the house until we've both calmed some."

"Yes, Pa," I said, turning to go and trying to keep down a smile. Never in a hundred years would I ever laugh at Pa when he was stirred up. But I'd never seen dirt all over his face, or dropping out of his hair, either, and he did look funny.

Press was sitting up in the bed Pa had pulled into the front of the house. He was reading when I came in.

Smirking at him, I said, "Are you comfortable?"

"Don't you look lovely, all hot and tired," he said.

"Oh, hush up. I wouldn't be like this if you did your share, would I?"

"All right, Sadie." He swung his left leg over the side of the bed and strained his face. "If you could . . . just help me . . . I'll try to get up."

"Oh, stop." I laughed and pushed him back to his pillow. Pulling the rocker closer, I snatched his book and sat back. "So, what are the feeble reading these days? *The Modern Prometheus**? What is that?"

"A novel," he said, taking it back. "Some of it is hard reading, but from what I can make out, this doctor fellow creates a demon out of parts from folks that have died, then brings him to life."

"That's terrible," I said. "Where'd you get such a thing?"

"Zeke brought it by yesterday. He said his Ma won't let him read novels. He brought it to me because she was about to burn it."

"I can see why. Put it away. Pa will have your hide if he finds you reading something like that."

"He won't, unless you tell him."

"Don't get me into this. You should be studying your spelling words, and you know it."

"I don't care what place I get in the match. I'm happy to be first out, and *you* know it. What's the matter with you, Sadie? You're going soft."*

"I am not. It's just . . . well, you didn't see Pa last week. He was so upset. It kinda made me want to do better."

"Do what better?" he said, looking disgusted.

"Preston, I'm trying not to get in any trouble. That's all."

"That's all? You may as well jump off the barn roof and put an end to it all right now. Holy smokes, Sadie. I never thought you'd turn on me."

"I haven't turned on anybody. I just . . ."

"Then swear you won't tell about the book."

"I don't care about your dumb old book."

"Then swear."

By the smirk on his face, I could see that he didn't expect me to do it. Then again, he did call me soft. I couldn't let him get away with that. Staring him straight in the eye, I said, "All right. I swear."

He stuffed the book under his pillow and said, "That's better."

Pa loaded the wagon full of regular potatoes  to sell in Salt Lake City and also a special batch that was close to perfect. He was taking them to the tithing office. Even Ma was surprised at that.

Thursday, just as they were leaving, Ma gave me a list of things to watch out for, as if I hadn't been living here all my life. I didn't need to be reminded to keep the lid on the flour barrel, or not to let the fire go out.

But it was a new thought having to gather the children for prayers, and to read the scriptures before bedtime. I wondered how Preston would take to all these changes.

Ma had all the regular chores on the list, too, and a reminder that Preston's work was now mine, along with the cooking, cleaning, and tending that she usually did.

I was about to get all bent out of shape over it when Ma said, "This will be the first real chance you've had to keep house by yourself."

I went red in the face, I know, but I liked her treating me this way—as if I was almost a grown lady.

She kissed the little children good-bye, then, taking my braid in her hand, said, "Twelve years old in a few weeks. You're growing up so quickly. I am very proud of you. Take care of everyone."

Pa helped her into the wagon and climbed in himself.

Ma waved to us until they came to the first turn, and then they were gone.

I put my arm around Ginny, who was wiping her eyes with her apron.

For some reason I was warmed with the feeling that maybe I *could* look after things on my own.

Jakey took my hand, saying, "When will Ma be back, Sadie?"

I twirled him around to face me. "She's hardly out of the yard, Jake. Are you missing her already?"

He kicked a couple of pebbles at his feet and nodded.

"It's all right," I said, looking down at him. "We're going to have fun, aren't we, Ginny?"

She stayed quiet, staring at the house.

There in the open doorway stood Preston with Zeke's crutch under his arm.

He smiled at me. "You bet we are."

CHAPTER SIX

Miscellaneous Mischief

"Preston Heber Russell!" I shouted. "What do you think you are doing?"

He just stood there, grinning.

"The doctor said you have to stay off that leg or it won't heal."

"I'm not on it," he said.

Going up the stairs, I took hold of his arm and pulled. "Go on. Lay back down before you hurt yourself."

"I'm not gonna hurt myself. I'm tired of laying around. I want to do something."

Ginny pled with him, too, but Jakey thought this was great fun. He danced around Press like he was a Maypole.

"Preston's better, better, better," he sang.

Preston loved the stir he was causing, mostly because he knew it was making me crazy.

"Look," I said, "Ma left me in charge. So don't you go doing anything nutty, or I'll be the one in trouble."

"Oh, you can be in charge, Sadie. That's fine by me. I won't get in your way."

I motioned for Ginny to get the rocker.

"Well, at least sit down then, before you fall."

She brought the chair, and I gave it a push toward him. He held up the crutch, turned on his good leg, and sat down.

I knew that most of what he did was to give us all a shock. Since Ma wasn't here, maybe he wanted to get me worked up instead. I figured the best way to deal with him was to not act surprised at whatever he did. I crossed my fingers, hoping that he wouldn't feel like pulling anything big on me.

As it turned out, he didn't need to.

The best part about being left in charge was that Ma didn't expect me to go to school. Of course, Ginny still had to, but as long as I could work on my spelling, I was glad to be home. I walked my sister halfway, then watched until she was out of sight. After all, I did have a household to see to.

By the time I got back, Preston had talked Jakey into trying to boil eggs. Of course, he couldn't even carry the kettle without sloshing the water all across the floor. It helped me stay calm when I remembered that I wanted to make Ma proud of me.

"Here, Jakey," I said. "Let me hang the kettle for you."

"Why? I'm big enough to do it," he said. "Press says so."

"Is that right?" I gave a mean smile to Preston.

He looked around the room, then back at me as if he had nothing to do with it.

"Well, little boys shouldn't play near the fire. You know that."

"I'm not little, and I wasn't playing. We want eggs for breakfast, that's all."

"What happened to the mush Ma already made?"

Preston started to whistle "Jimmy Crack Corn."

"We didn't want it, so I threw it out," Jakey said.

"You what?" I asked. "Jakey, we don't waste good food. What did you really do with it?"

The whistling got louder.

Jakey pointed to the porch.

Realizing what he meant, I said, "You didn't. Preston, did you tell him to take it out?"

It was easy to see that he thought this was funny—wasting food—when just last year the grasshoppers had left us almost nothing to eat at all. Ma would go wild if she found out.

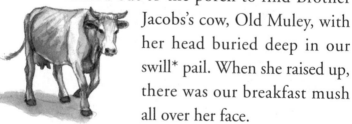

I hurried out to the porch to find Brother Jacobs's cow, Old Muley, with her head buried deep in our swill* pail. When she raised up, there was our breakfast mush all over her face.

"Shoo! You rotten thing," I said, flapping my apron at her. There she stood, chewing away, not the least bit afraid of me or my apron.

Back inside, I mopped up the floor while the

eggs cooked over the fire. After they had boiled a good ten minutes, I let them cool, then shelled and mashed them with a fork. The entire time it took to cook and clean up, I didn't say a word to anyone. Preston wasn't going to get to me so soon.

"Old Muley came back today," I said later, making light conversation to show that I wasn't at all ruffled.

"Yeah, she shows up every morning," he said. "Sometimes I'd like to take a stick to her and chase her home. One of these days I will."

By the time Ginny came back from school, I'd done everything I could think of inside and was very ready to get to the outside chores.

Keeping Press in bed had been the hardest thing of all, and I had even made bread. Stew was bubbling over the fire, but the potatoes were still hard and shiny, so there was plenty of time to take care of the yard work.

Pa would have had the stalls dug out by early morning, but he didn't have a troublesome invalid and a five-year-old to look after. Ginny and I milked the cows and fed the pigs, though there wasn't much left in the swill pail for them to eat, thanks to the Jacobses' cow.

Nearer to suppertime, Preston said, "The stew looks too thin. Maybe you should add more flour."

"Are you going to tell me how to cook now?" I asked.

He made a sad face, pretending he had his feelings hurt, and said, "I was only trying to help."

Thinking for one second that he was serious, I almost apologized. I'm glad I didn't.

As I went to add more flour to the stew, I found that the lid that normally rests on top of the barrel rim had been pushed down too far. It was stuck tight.

I'd seen Ma get it out before with just a few taps on one side with a knife handle. That seemed easy enough, but with each tap, the lid seemed more firm than ever.

If Preston hadn't worn me ragged all day hopping himself around one minute, then making me wait on him the next, I may have asked for his advice.

Seeing that he had fallen asleep anyhow, I tried sliding the knife under the edge of the lid. It moved just enough to encourage me, so I held it steady with one hand and pounded it down with the other. No sooner had I stabbed the knife alongside of the wooden circle than it broke free. The lid plunged into the barrel, sending a thick cloud of smoky-white flour puffing into my face.

My first thought was relief that at least Press didn't see that.

But before I could blink the flour out of my eyes, a raft of laughter broke out from the corner of the room.

When I could finally see, there sat Preston, Jake, and even Ginny busting out in hysterics at the whole joke, obviously put together by our dear little sufferer.

Realizing then how Ma comes across her temper, I wanted to throw more than the mush stick at all of them. The whole day's anger was boiling in a way that should have worried Preston.

Just as I looked the room over for some way to hush them up, I caught a glance of myself in the reflecting glass.*

My brown hair, face, and neck were dusted white, and each time I moved, powder fluttered down from my eyelashes like a tiny winter storm.

I couldn't do anything but laugh at myself. Then it dawned on me that maybe the other children were tired of being so clean.

So, walking carefully to Preston's bedside, I said, "Merry Christmas, everyone."

With that, I shook like a dog.

CHAPTER SEVEN

Lady of the House

Thinking it would calm everyone down if we read the scriptures like Ma had wanted, I asked Preston to do it. To my surprise, he said yes without much of a fuss. The problem was that he wanted to recite the shortest scripture verse that he could find, rather than read for a few minutes. Being that this was new to all of us, I let him have his way.

He stood up with the Book of Mormon in one hand and said, "And my father dwelt in a tent."

I don't have to say that it didn't calm anyone down. Once everyone had stopped laughing, I asked Ginny to say the prayer. She did real good, too, even with Jake and Press jabbing at each other the whole way through.

We went to bed that night filled to the brim with warm stew and bread. The house was a shambles from our playing, but I knew we had the next two days to clean it up, so it wasn't a worry.

At least not until I came downstairs the next

morning and found the flour barrel full of mice. They always come in the house this time of year to get out of the cold, which is fine—if you like mice. But when there is food laying around, or in this case, an open flour barrel, they can really be a pesky trial.

Ma hated mice more than wolves and almost as much as crickets. She was always saying that mice would like to take rule of the whole world, but they wouldn't have her place—not if she could help it. It sure was a good thing that she wasn't here to see them with full run of the kitchen.

It made me sick to watch the little gray beasts scurrying around in our food. So, without a second thought, I grabbed up one of Ma's pie pans and banged it with a wooden spoon, loud enough to wake the dead, or even Preston.

The noise, I was pleased to find, rattled him out of his dreams and nearly out of the bed. The good thing was that the mice jumped from the barrel and went out a knothole in the side wall before Preston saw that they were there. It wouldn't be hard to stop up the hole later, when no one was looking.

Hearing the clatter, my brother sat straight up in bed as if he'd been shot. He scowled at me, but I smiled as sweetly as I could.

"Time to get up, dear brother."

He laid back down and covered his head with the blanket, saying, "So we're even now. One trick deserves one, I guess."

"How true," I said, feeling triumphant.

That is, until I noticed that in my exhaustion the night before, I hadn't piled the coals the way I should have. Now we had no fire, and the ashes were cold. It was a humiliating thought to imagine walking up to Sister Carter and asking for a fire start.*

In the end, I decided to take the bake kettle*

all the way to the Jacobses' place. That way I could get the live embers *and* bring their cow back to them.

I hid Preston's crutch, hoping that he'd be less trouble to me if I could keep him still. But he got up first thing and just hopped around without it. And when he went out to the porch, he looked so wobbly to me that I got scared he'd hurt himself and gave the crutch back.

It seemed to make him crazy to be cooped up inside like an old hen. I hoped that as long as he didn't touch his bad foot to the ground, it would be all right. He was a hard one to keep tied down. It made me wonder if even Ma could do it.

Ginny brought the corner chair outside for him to sit on, but he said he was going for a walk.

"It better be a hop," I said, trying to be funny.

As he started down the side of the house, he said, "I'll be just fine."

I stood with my hands on my hips, shaking my head. "I can't worry about him. I have a household to run."

"You look just like Ma," Jakey said, taking my hand.

For some reason, that made me feel good.

"Spell *tabernacle.*" Ginny grinned at me.

"Come help me clean inside," I said, "and I'll spell any word you can say."

I used to wonder why Ma always tidied up and did the dishes at night instead of waiting until morning. It wasn't hard to figure out once we were the ones doing the washing. The pans and bowls had so much stew left and dried on them that we had to let them soak a full hour before we could get them clean.

When Preston came back inside, his face was all gray, and he was out of breath. I figured it served him right for not minding the doctor, and if he took sick from too much exertion*—well, he brought it on himself. Without saying anything, he made it over to the bed and climbed in. The next time I looked, he was asleep.

I was proud of the way things were straightening up, so after we put Jakey down for a nap, I decided to try my hand at making a vinegar pie.* The crust was crooked and browned too fast, but it looked good enough to make me proud.

While it cooled, Ginny and I went out to see to the animals.

"Brother Jacobs must have tied up Old Muley today," I said. "We have a full bucket for the pigs."

Preston paid for his little jaunt by being too tired to get up the rest of the day. I made meat pies for supper, but when Jakey took him his plate, he just turned away. That had me worried. Any time Preston Russell will refuse food, the steeple is in a blaze.*

I pulled the corner chair closer to his bed, turning so that I could still get the glow from the fireplace while I mended his torn shirt. Ma didn't need any more reminders of *that day,* so I tried to make it look the best I could, hoping we could all just forget about it.

Preston rolled over. For a minute it looked like he had been crying. I knew that couldn't be. Fourteen-year-old boys who are made of bear hide don't cry much.

"Your leg hurt?" I asked.

He stared straight ahead. "Not too bad."

"Do you need anything?"

"You don't know, Sadie."

"Know what?" I couldn't tell if something hurt or if he was sick.

"Preston, are you all right? Should I send for the doctor?"

"No, he can't help." His voice had a mournful sound that I hadn't heard from him before.

Water, I thought. *Maybe he needs a drink.* I went to the bucket outside and dipped out a cupful of water, but when I offered it to him, he pushed it away.

"What's wrong, Press?"

He turned his head from me. "I've done something. Something terrible."

"You wouldn't know how to do something really terrible. What, did you lose Zeke's demon book?"

"No, it's not that."

Putting my hand on his shoulder, I said, "Look, it can't be that bad."

"It is, Sadie."

"Tell me, then."

"I can't."

Just then, Ginny and Jake came in, all dirty

from playing outside in the barn. I tried to shoo them back out to wash up, but it wasn't easy. When I finally got them cleaned, Preston was curled next to the wall and asleep again. Whatever was bothering him had let go, at least for now.

"Ginny," I said, watching my brother sleep, "brighten the fire, would you?"

She pulled a handful of sagebrush from the tinderbox* and tossed it onto the flames. Instantly, the fire leaped up and lit the room nearly to daylight. I chewed my lip, thinking and worrying for Press, then took up my needle again.

CHAPTER EIGHT

The Reformation

On the day Ma and Pa were to return, Dr. Dunyon came by to look in on Preston. He was surprised to find him in bed and acting so tired. There was no hiding that he'd been up a bit, because he had hay stuck to the bottom of his foot. The doctor just made a clicking noise with his tongue when he saw it, then gave him some medicine for the pain. It was supposed to help him sleep, besides.

As he pulled away in his buggy, I wanted to yell that we didn't need Press to sleep anymore. We needed to know what had made him so upset yesterday.

"Spell *medicine*," Ginny said.

I closed my eyes and said, low, "Not now, Ginny."

Ma and Pa rode in at about half past four. Jakey nearly got run over by the wagon for trying to get to Ma before it stopped.

Of course, Ginny was so excited that she started to cry.

I was happy to see them—and even more happy to turn Ma's house back over to her.

"The place looks good," Ma said. "I see you all survived. How did you like taking on a household, Sadie?"

"It sure fills up your mind every minute, doesn't it?"

Pa laughed.

"That it does," Ma said.

"We would have been home earlier this afternoon, but we were stopped in town by quite a ruckus,"* Pa said. "Maybe you already know."

I looked at Ginny. We both shook our heads.

"We didn't get the whole story, but it seems that someone killed the Jacobses' cow."

"Old Muley?" I couldn't believe it. "Why?"

"No one knows. They just found her in the

yard dead. Somehow she was wounded, but she made her way home before she died."

"Old Muley was a pest," I said, "but no one wanted to hurt her."

"It's a mystery," Pa said, shaking his head.

Ma spoke up. "We really have happier news to tell you than that, don't we, Solomon?"

"Yes, we do." He took Ma's hand and patted it. "Go ahead, dear."

"No, I think you should."

"All right, then."

Jakey, watching Pa and Ma acting so sweet, started to giggle.

I shook my head at him so he'd stop, but he didn't. We'd never seen them be so friendly to each other. I liked it.

Pa stood up. "Family, there is a great movement going through this church which affects us all. President Young and his counselors have been feeling the same frustration that I have felt lately. There are too many people in this valley who have forgotten how to live the gospel principles.

"Our prophet spoke to us and made it quite clear that we are to do better. We are to make right all the wrongs we've done and repay our debts. No more whitewashing."*

I swallowed, wondering if this was leading up to a story about swiping a neighbor's apples.

Ma said, "Children, it was really wonderful. The meeting reminded me of the old revivals my family went to when I was a little girl. The singing, the fire in the speaker's voice, the thrill of hoping to be free from all our sins."

Ginny got so caught up in what Ma and Pa were telling us that she sat pressing her hands together as if any second she was gonna start clapping.

"The Spirit was so strong," Pa said, "that we were nearly overwhelmed. President Young's counselor Jedediah Grant said that the Lord wanted us to pledge ourselves to the cause of righteousness just like the people of King Benjamin did in the Book of Mormon."

Ma leaned forward and put her hand on my shoulder. "Sadie," she said, "it was as though we were hearing the gospel for the first time. Why, I felt as if we were trading in our old souls for a set of new ones."

There was a strange excitement working through me, too, as I listened. It had my stomach jumping like I'd swallowed a couple of brook minnows. The idea of having a new, clean soul made my heart race within my ribs.

"Your father and I have been talking the entire way home about the changes we want to make."

"I, for one," Pa said, "Have made a vow to be a better leader in this home. I will see to it that we have scripture reading and prayers every evening and get to our Sabbath meetings on Sunday. No excuses."

"I have pledged to see that we are better neighbors," Ma took courage with a wink from Pa, "and to control my temper."

Though I wasn't sure that Preston would have liked the conversation, I wished he would wake up to see Ma and Pa so thrilled. It would have to cheer him.

Pa walked over to the sideboard* and lifted up my pie.

"What is this? Edith, did you sneak home and bake this lovely pie while I wasn't looking?"

Ma patted my knee.

"I know my little Sadie couldn't have done it," he said, cutting a piece for himself and one for Ma.

I looked at the floor and grinned.

"Anyway," Ma said, "all this won't be easy, but we can do it. Your Pa and I agree that one of the most important things we can teach you children is to always be honest."

Pa nodded. "It's the only way to breathe fresh air."*

There was a small movement at the side of the room.

Ma looked over, saying, "Preston, good. You're awake."

CHAPTER NINE

The Crime

Preston must have gotten over whatever was troubling him, because he didn't bring it up again, and when I did, he said, "I was just tired. It was nothing."

Before our folks had been home three days, Pa was called to be a block teacher* for our neighborhood. The bishop gave him and his partner, Brother Fletcher, a list of questions that they were to ask folks as they went from house to house on "their block."

Ma and Pa thought it would be good to ask their own family the same questions before Pa went out nudging others to be better people. He sat us all at the table, even Preston.

"Some of these we'll have to think heavily about," Pa said. "Then others don't really apply."

Ma, who wanted to make sure we were being fair to everyone, said, "Of course, they all apply. Go ahead, Solomon. Read us *all* the questions."

"All right, Edie. If you're sure. First question. 'Have you committed murder?'"

"Solomon!" Ma said, "What on earth are you saying?"

"Well, now, Edie, I warned you."

"Fine, fine. Read us the ones that you think apply."

Pa grinned and went on. "'Have you taken property not your own?'" Both he and Ma looked at me.

I said, "Preston is feeling much better now. Maybe we could give him some of the blame."

"Me?" he said. "I was just following you. As always."

I nudged him with my elbow. "That's a fib. Pa, are you going to ask anything about fibbing?"

"You two do need to find a way to repay the Carters for the apples you've taken over the last while," Ma said. "If you want to right your wrongs, you should start there."

"Yes, Ma," I said.

Preston just smiled like he was obedient or something.

Ginny didn't like us talking about the apples. It made her mad all over again that she had believed us.

"'Have you turned your animals into another person's field without his consent?' That one's for me, I suppose," Pa said. "We lost the animals, so in a way we paid for the grain."

Jakey asked, "What's that mean?" every few minutes. Once in a while, Ma would try to explain. Sometimes she couldn't without interrupting Pa.

"That isn't fair," Preston said. "How can you worry about right and wrong and just let Brother Richardson steal some of our animals?"

"It isn't fair, son," Pa said. "But it feels right to let Brother Richardson use his own conscience to solve this one. If I do anything else, it will just make an enemy out of him. It isn't worth that to me."

"If he's stealing your stock, then he's already an enemy."

"Sometimes people don't think they are stealing," Ma said in a soft voice.

Preston sat scowling like this meant a lot to him.

"'Have you lied about any person or thing?'" Preston sighed.

I knew that look. He was getting impatient with all this "becoming better people" talk.

Pa went on with the questions for some time. He asked about returning what we borrow, taking the Lord's name in vain, keeping the Sabbath day holy, coveting, and paying tithing.

When he came to the question, "Have you found lost property and not returned it to the owner?" Preston took up his crutch and went out the door.

"Preston, come back," Pa said.

He looked back with a deep sadness on his face and just closed the door behind him.

There was a time, most of my life, in fact, when he and I were so close that there wasn't anything we couldn't tell each other. I've always known him. Why did he think that I wouldn't understand what was in his mind now?

When Brother Fletcher came to work the neighborhood with Pa, he brought a plate of ginger cake for Preston from Pearly. From what I could see, he didn't care who it came from. Food was food. He told Brother Fletcher "thanks," and then it took about two minutes for the cake to disappear.

In some ways, Preston was the same as always, but there was something different about him that I couldn't figure. Like the light in his eyes wasn't there anymore. It made me sad to watch him this way.

I sat on the porch with Press, not saying a word, when the men came home. Pa went right inside to tell Ma the news. We listened through the open door. He told her that Brother Carter was very sick, but it wasn't a body sickness. It was more of an illness of the heart, he said.

"Apparently, the bishop and his counselors looked into the death of the Jacobses' cow and decided that Brother Carter must have done it."

"What?" Ma said. "He can't even work in the yard. How would he hurt that cow?"

"He says he didn't do it, poor man. But the animal died of a cut in his side, and the trail went from Carter's yard to the Jacobs family's yard."

"Poor Muley," I whispered.

"Quiet," Preston snapped. He never would have done that before.

"Anyway," Pa said, "Brother Carter had to pay for the cow or . . ."

"Or what?" Ma asked.

"Or face being disfellowshipped."

Ma gasped. "And he paid?"

"Said the Lord knows he didn't do it, but if everyone else thinks he did, then he has no choice. His membership in the Church means that much to him."

Preston doubled his hand into a fist and slammed it into the porch post. "No!" he said through his teeth.

Pa must have heard him, and he looked through the doorway at us, wondering.

I couldn't stand it anymore. "Preston," I

touched his arm, "what's happening to you? Why won't you talk to me?"

He pulled away. For the first time since I was a little girl, I started to cry.

Back then, he would've run off, refusing to stay near a "weeping woman." But now he stared out to the fields like his heart was breaking. Finally, he said, "Don't you understand, Sadie?"

"No," I cried, "I don't."

He came a step closer. "This is all my fault. *I killed Muley.*"

CHAPTER TEN

Resolution

Ma and Pa must have sensed Preston's suffering. Or maybe they heard me crying. Whichever way, they came slowly to the porch and stood quiet while he rambled on through his story.

"It was an accident," he said. "I was just trying to chase her back home. She was in Brother Carter's yard when it happened."

Preston pushed his hair back from his forehead. If it had been easier for him to walk, he would have been pacing back and forth across the porch. He needed me to be quiet and just listen; so I sat still, afraid that if I moved, it would break the spell and he would stop talking again.

"I couldn't walk fast enough to scare her, so I got a stick from the side yard and . . . well, you know how I always said I was going to throw a stick at her. That's what I did. It landed at her feet, and she reared sideways, crashing into the woodpile."

He rubbed his hands hard on his pant legs and looked at me, then Ma. Pa stared at the ground. Preston's eyes were big and dark, like he'd had no sleep in days.

I knew he wanted to cry too, like me. He already had, that day last week when it happened. But today, it was as if he had to tell us what he'd been holding in for so long. Now that he'd started, he couldn't stop.

"I knew she was hurt bad, but I had no way to get to her. She took off into the pasture behind Carters' and headed toward home. That's when I saw it."

He waited, biting at the side of his lip, and staring off at nothing.

"What?" I whispered.

"Sadie, I'd never hurt that old stupid cow." Glancing again at Ma, then me, he asked, "You know that, don't you?"

I sniffed hard and wiped at the tears running down my face. Giving him a sad smile, I nodded.

He closed his eyes for just a second, then whispered, "Sadie, the ax was wedged in with the firewood." Pa opened his mouth but nothing came out. Ma covered her face with her hands.

"Oh, Preston," I cried.

My poor brother turned to face Pa and said, "I can always think my way out of trouble, but I can't fix this. There just isn't a way to. It's too much. Brother Carter is liable to die from all this. And it's my fault."

He looked frantic, like he was being chased by something bigger than all of us.

Coming right up to his boy, Pa grabbed Preston's shoulders and pulled him close. "It's right that you told us, son. I'm proud you did."

"But you can't tell, Pa—you can't!"

"Oh, I won't," he said. "I swear."

I couldn't believe my ears. Ma was looking puzzled, too. Preston leaned back and stared into Pa's face. "You mean it?"

"Of course I mean it. I swear I won't tell the

bishop, the Carters, or the Jacobses . . . because *you* have to tell them."

Preston jerked around and glared at Pa. "What?"

"That's right," he said. "It's the only way. You said it yourself. This is too big to figure out alone. And we can't just leave it. Trading in our old ways—remember? We're going to do the right thing."

Preston tried to argue but finally closed his eyes and nodded. Pa patted his arm and said, "Come on, son."

Preston sat back in the meadow grass reading the grammar book. "Spell *confession*."

"C-O-N-F-E-S-S-I-O-N," I said, from the high branch of the apple tree. "It would be much easier to do this if you would try to catch these."

"All right, all right," he said, rising to his feet. "I've picked everything in my reach." Then, making like he was about to climb up after me on his one good leg, "But if you want . . ."

"No, no," I said, laughing. "Stay there. I'll do the climbing this time. But if you're not careful, something might fall out of the sky and hit you on the head."

"Believe it or not, I think something already did. Spell *reform*."

"R-E-F-O-R-M."

Pa walked up, lugging a full bushel basket, and set it down by the others.

Jakey, with an apple in each hand, said, "Pa says I've picked enough to pay for Muley all by myself."

Pa winked at me.

After Preston and Pa had a meeting with Brother Carter, Brother Jacobs, and the bishop, things felt much better for everyone. Brother Carter had already paid for Muley, so he said if our family would glean* his apples and help him get them to market, he'd be more than repaid for the cow *and* the apples Preston and I took.

We all agreed that it was the least we could do.

Ma said it was the most neighborly thing.

"Don't get too high now, Sadie," Pa said. "I'm not wanting to have any more broken bones in the family."

From one of the other trees, Ginny called, "Pa! Ma and I have another bushel for you."

"Be right there." Patting Preston on the back, he said, "How do you feel, son?"

"Better than I have in a long time. It must be all this fresh air."

Pa threw back his head and laughed. "Must be, son. Must be."

All I know is that Preston finally had that look back in his eyes. That look we all love and wouldn't trade for the world.

GLOSSARY
In Sadie's Own Words

bake kettle—A big pot for cooking soup or stew. Ma even made cornbread in it sometimes. **See page 45.**

"Big Match"—The biggest spelling bee of the year. It happens in late October. **See page 3.**

block teacher—A church calling where the brother goes to the homes of his neighbors to make sure that everything is all right. **See page 57.**

bootjack—A two-pronged iron fork used to hold onto your boot while you pull your foot out of it. **See page 23.**

breathe fresh air—It's part of an old saying: "Being honest is the only way to breathe fresh air." It means to have a clear conscience. **See page 56.**

castoff fruit—The fruit that had already fallen to the ground. **See page 9.**

crook—A sharp, V-shaped bend in the tree. **See page 10.**

exertion—Working very hard. **See page 47.**

fire start—Live coals to get a fire going with. **See page 45.**

garret—The attic, or a space under the roof. **See page 2.**

glean—To harvest grain or fruit when it's ripe. **See page 68.**

half again as big—I meant that Preston's foot was swollen bigger than its normal size. **See page 17.**

husk mattress—A mattress stuffed with shredded corn husks. **See page 14.**

likely—Healthy and strong. **See page 4.**

making a ruckus—Making noise and horsing around. **See page 52.**

mauled—We looked like we'd been attacked by a wild animal. **See page 11.**

The Modern Prometheus—The first title to the book *Frankenstein* by Mary Shelley, written in 1818. Ma and Pa would never have allowed Press to read a time-wasting novel—especially about a monster who killed people. **See page 30.**

mush stick—A carved wooden stick used for stirring porridge and mush. **See page 6.**

no better than a load of firewood—Ma meant we were sitting around doing nothing. **See page 4.**

poultice—A mixture of warm wet herbs wrapped in cloth. It's used to bring down the swelling or to fight off infection. **See page 18.**

redding up—Getting ripe. **See page 7.**

reflecting glass—A mirror. **See page 41.**

rheumatism—Pain in the muscles and joints. **See page 21.**

shell—To take all the corn off the cob once it is dried. **See page 25.**

sideboard—The flat working space below Ma's cupboard, where she chops, kneads, and fixes our meals. **See page 55.**

soft—Preston meant that I didn't want to be adventurous anymore, because I was too afraid of getting into trouble. **See page 31.**

spitfire—Someone who's got a quick temper. **See page 5.**

steeple is in a blaze—That means that it's easy to see that something is wrong. **See page 48.**

swill—The scraps of food we don't eat. We usually feed the swill to the pigs. **See page 38.**

tinderbox—A box by the side of the fireplace that holds kindling wood. **See page 50.**

tirade—A long speech where someone gets very worked up. **See page 3.**

vinegar pie—A nasty sounding pie that is truly a sweet-tasting custard in a flaky crust. **See page 47.**

whitewashing—Covering up the truth or pretending you don't have any faults. **See page 54.**

WHAT REALLY HAPPENED

During the years 1856 and 1857, the Church experienced a recommitment to living the gospel that was known as the Mormon Reformation. President Brigham Young issued a call to all members to reform their lives. They were to make right their wrongs, forgive one another, and, in general, try to do better. Special meetings were held throughout the Church to help people repent and become converted to the gospel once again. The phrases "Saints, do your duty," "Live your religion," and "Be ye perfect" were used by leaders to encourage the people to have a greater commitment to righteousness.

Jedediah M. Grant, second counselor to President Young, went about "preaching, baptizing, exhorting from morning until night, day after day, . . . to promote the spiritual welfare of his people" (Orson F. Whitney, *History of Utah*, 4 vols. [Salt Lake City: George Q. Cannon &

Sons, 1892], 1:565). He truly wore out his life for the cause. He caught a severe cold and on Monday, December 1, 1856, he died, having "shed forth the steady and brilliant light of lofty and correct example" (see *Millennial Star,* 19:185; 42:755). Jedediah M. Grant was the father of Heber J. Grant, seventh president of the Church.

ABOUT THE AUTHOR

When Launi Anderson was approached with the idea of writing books for the Latter-day Daughters Series, she balked. "I only write picture books," she said. With more than 25,000 copies of her novels sold, she has proven that she can, indeed, write for the 8- to 12-year-old audience.

Launi is the mother of five children, April, Lyndi, Jillian, Dane, and Rhen. She has adopted a dog and owns an assortment of cats and one hedgehog.

Launi has had many callings in the Church. She says that one of the things she enjoys doing most is LDS historical research.

Not only does Launi write and play with her kids, but she also enjoys music, cooking, storytelling, organizing, and chatting. She is clever, witty, and a blast to be around. If you need a good laugh, find Launi. She's my friend.

Love,
Carol

From *Clarissa's Heart*
Another Exciting New Title
in the Latter-day Daughters Series

Just then, the captain of our handcart company
called a rest halt.

I reached up to touch the necklace at my throat.
After a second or two, my fingers found the chain,
but the carved shell—the pelican—was gone!
Holding out my skirt, I tried to see if maybe the
little bird was stuck in the mud caked on my dress.
I ran my hands over the fabric, but it was not there.

If it had come off while we were pushing the
cart, it could be buried in the wet ground, maybe a
foot deep.

In my mind I saw Eli, his eyes as blue as the
ocean. Feeling complete despair, I slid down and sat
beside the handcart, trying my best not to cry.